Footprints, Umbrellas, Noodles & more...

POEMS FOR CHILDREN
Volume I

Janet Clough

Written by Janet Dixon Clough
Illustrated by Jennifer Savage Britton

† Attributions

AUTHORS, card game, copyright 1987, U.S. Games Systems, Inc., Stamford, CT 06902 USA

SORRY, board game – The Game of Sweet Revenge, Parker Brothers, 2005 Hasbro, Pawtucket, RI 02862. All Rights Reserved. TM and ® denote U.S. Trademarks.

CANDYLAND, board game – The World of Sweets, 2010 Hasbro, Pawtucket, RI 02862 USA. All Rights Reserved. TM and ® denote U.S. Trademarks. MB Games.Candyland.com

• •

Text and illustrations copyright 2011 by Janet Dixon Clough

www.dixonliterature.com

Creative Direction by **Eddie King**

Front Cover & Interior Illustrations by **Jennifer Savage Britton**, as well as *Book Layout*

All rights reserved. No part of this publication may be reproduced, stored in a retrieval system, or transmitted in any form or by any means – electronic, mechanical, photocopy, recording or any other – except brief quotations in printed review, without the written permission of the author.

PRINTED AND BOUND IN THE UNITED STATES OF AMERICA.

ISBN: 978-0-9848377-0-0

Acknowledgements

Our Heavenly Father, for making all things possible.

Jennifer Savage Britton, for her delightful and insightful illustrations.

Eddie King, for his wisdom, guidance, friendship, and everlasting support.

Mary Wherry, for her tireless ear and her support of this project.

Joann Tomlin (FA), *Favorite Aunt* for her creative suggestions, her love and belief in me.

All the family members, friends, neighbors, pets and critters that gave me inspiration.

Table of Contents

Melody Mouse..6

Me and My Bike...8

Noodles...10

My Garden..12

Wind..14

Books..16

Spider..18

Games...20

Little Betty Bunny...22

The Post Lady..24

Raindrops...26

Spring..28

Squirrel..30

Molly by the Sea..32

Yoga...34

Stars...36

Tilley, My Dog..38

Umbrellas...40

Fruits...42

Off To the Beach..44

Halloween..46

Kyle's Bags..48

Little Puppy...50

Mary's Griddle...52

The Screen Door..54

Footprints...56

Lancer...58

St. Patrick's Day..60

Ricky Raccoon..62

Cluffy...64

Melody Mouse ate some cheese
And before she knew it,
She started to sneeze.

She loved her cheese and crusty bread
But when she nibbled,
Her nose turned bright red.

She wondered and wondered
What step she could take
Then quickly decided to just eat cupcakes.

Melody Mouse

Me and My Bike

I rode my bike
A long, long way.
It was such a warm and sunny day.

> Over the hills and through the fields,
> I peddled and pumped
> Until my legs squealed.

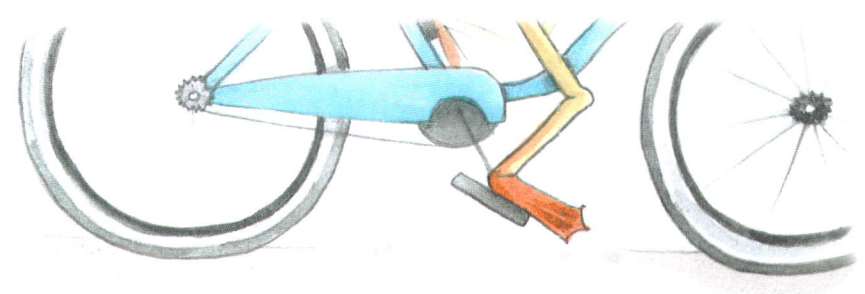

Then I coasted and rested and finally slowed down.
I smiled and cruised
Back into town.

           Oh, what a day this was…so full of fun!
           Just me and my bike
           Out for a run.

Noodles

I love to eat noodles…they are so good!
Mom likes them too
And calls them comfort food.

Some are long and some are curly.
Some are short, some twisted,
And some can be eaten in a hurry.

All noodles, no matter what size or shape,
Are always as slippery
As a wet little snake.

Spaghetti, rigatoni, penne, and bow tie…
All slide right down.
You don't even have to try.

My Garden

Spring is coming very soon.
The grass is green
And the trees are in bloom.

Spring means time to dig in the dirt,
Plant veggies, and flowers
…a lot of work!

It's worth all the trouble when things start to grow.
The flowers are pretty
And the veggies…..oh ho!

The radishes, lettuce, and peppers, too
Make more than enough
For me and you.

I love to share all that I grow
With neighbors and friends,
Even folks I don't know.

There's too much food for me to eat
So come to my garden
And I'll give you a treat.

Wind

The *wind* is howling through the trees.
The leaves are rustling
In the strong breeze.

It makes my skin tingle and hair stand on end.
The chair in my yard
Is about to upend.

When the *wind* is wild and makes all feel eerie,
I'm glad when it passes
And all's again cheery.

Books

Books are very special friends
That can take you to
Far, far away lands.

They teach all subjects you should know
And tell all about
Places you should go.

Numbers and letters and flowers and trees,
Birds and fruits
And bumble bees….

Airplanes and trains and poems and such
Are all found in books
Oh, there's just so much!

So never forget your books are your friends
For much of your learning
Depends on them.

Spider

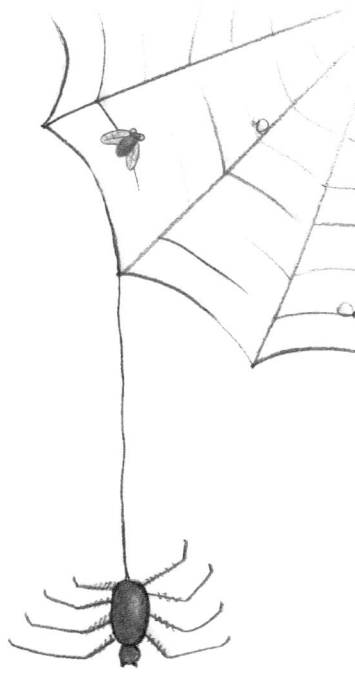

I wish I was a spider so I could creep and crawl
With long thin hairy legs,
Eight of them in all.

I'd spin a pretty web made of silky thread
Until I was so tired
I'd have to go to bed.

As I'd sleep on my little leaf bed,
The dew would fall silently
On my web.

In the night, a fly would buzz by
Land in my web
And start to cry.

I'd wake up then and welcome him,
Tell him not to be scared,
We would be good friends.

We'd play in the web that was covered in dew,
Get our feet wet
And not know what to do.

Before the day would come to an end,
I'd have to get busy
And spin again.

Games

Authors, Sorry, and Candyland †
Are my favorite games
In all the land.

Hours and hours, I can sit and *play*
Learning the rules
As I go on my way.

Mom and Dad think they let me win
But I know better,
I beat them!

Little Betty Bunny

Little Betty Bunny scampers along the dewy grass.
She nibbles the veggies and eats the stems
Of everything she happens to pass.

She's frightened when she hears my dog bark.
She runs and hides
Somewhere in the dark.

Under the basil, parsley, and mace…
Who knew that would be
Her hiding place?

Her little body snuggles down.
She's under the plants
And close to the ground.

I reach for an herb and feel her fur.
She doesn't mean to…
But scares me for sure!

Betty Bunny needs to eat and thrive.
Munching on my plants
Will keep her alive.

The Post Lady

The post lady comes in her big white truck
Bringing mail, magazines,
Advertisements, and such.

When she's hungry, she comes up to my door
To see if I have the tuna
That she adores.

I fix her a sandwich, iced tea, and some chips.
Then we talk and laugh while
She munches and sips.

It's fun to see her every day.
It's just not the same
When she's away.

Raindrops

Raindrops falling, p
                        i
                         t
                          t
                           e
                        r
                                 p
                                  a
                                  t
                                   t
                                   e
                                   r

Make me wonder
What's the matter?

Is an angel crying down?
Or a cloud
Making a frown?

Drops of rain on all the flowers
Make them grow
And give them powers.

God sends the rain for all to share...
And to let us know
How much he cares.

Spring

The spring is welcomed by one and all.
It means there will be
No more snowfall.

The breeze is warm and the smells are sweet,
And springtime flowers
Are such a treat.

Tulips, daffodils and pretty crocus
Pop up early and are
Everyone's focus.

Their colors are bright and their shapes are *pretty*;
So nice to enjoy as you
Move about the city.

Squirrel

The little squirrel in my backyard
Runs and jumps and
Plays so hard!

He hangs on the birdfeeder upside down
And sends all the birds
Flitting to the ground.

He eats all the bird food and never stops
Until it is gone and
The feeder's missing its top.

Molly By The Sea

Molly sat beside the sea.
Her toes in the sand,
Hair flying in the breeze.

Watching the wind blow
The grains of sand,
She wondered where each one would land.

Some in the sea oats and some on the beach
For sure, none would
Ever be hers to reach.

Yoga

Yoga is a way of life
That gives you balance
And eases strife.

Down dog, tree, and mountain pose
Are some asanas
Students should know.

Everyone likes to work on the mats,
Using the bricks
And long purple straps.

Stretching, bending, and forward folds,
Lengthening and broadening
Are worthy goals.

Heating poses and cooling ones too
Get the body
Into its groove.

Stars

I squint my eyes and I can see
A make-believe sky
Up over me.

The stars are sprinkled in this sky of mine.
They wink and twinkle
And really shine.

I'd like to put one in my pocket.
The way it sparkles,
It could go in my locket.

But I'll leave them in the sky tonight
So everyone can
Enjoy their sight.

Tilley, My Dog

Little Tilley took a nap

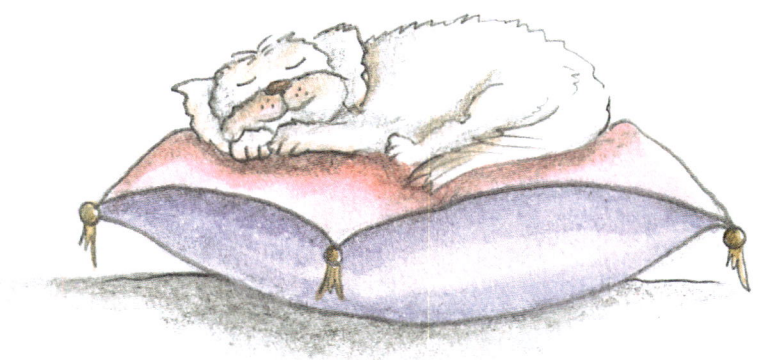

And dreamed she had wings
That she could flap.

Her wings took her up and very high,
So she could see
All the stars in the sky.

She flew and flew all over the place
And came upon an angel,
Face-to-face.

The angel had never seen a dog in flight
And Tilley gave her
Quite a fright.

Tilley's paw and the angel's hand
Joined tightly and
They became best friends.

Soon it was time for Tilley to wake
So she landed and
Gave herself a good shake.

Umbrellas

Bright umbrellas are sprinkled on the beach
Giving color and life to
Everyone they greet.

They flap and wave as the breeze whips up,
Then droop and fall
When the wind doesn't puff.

They keep the sun from burning your face.
Under the umbrella's
A cozy place.

Fruits

Apples, oranges, bananas, and grapes
Are good to eat and
Make you feel great.

The colors are bright and make you feel light.
Red, orange, green, and yellow
Can only make you a happy fellow.

Off to the Beach

We're going to the beach today.
We'll stop for gas
And to eat along the way.

Arriving there while the sun's still bright,
We'll play in the surf
'Til it's almost night.

The waves come crashing onto the beach
Where the sand is white
And soft as a peach.

Tomorrow I'll have to build a sand fort,
Make it tall and strong
With lots of support.

I don't want the waves to wash it away
But rather to let it
Stand there all day.

Halloween

Pumpkins and scarecrows and scary black cats…
Ghosts and witches with
Big pointy hats.

Costumes and children that go trick-or-treat
For lollipops, candy,
All things good to eat.

This is the most fun I've ever seen!
My favorite night……..
It's Halloween.

Kyle's Bags

Kyle has lots of pretty bags to carry her things in.
They're solids, plaids, and flowers,
Greens, yellows, tans.

Some have zippers; some have snaps;
Some have big
Fold over flaps.

Kyle's chic and cool and always ready.
I love her bags.
They are so pretty!

Little Puppy

Little puppy is acting sick.
Hope he hasn't been
Bitten by a tick.

He just won't eat and sleeps all day.
He doesn't even
Want to play.

The doctor gave him some big green pills.
I hope they take away
All his ills.

'Cause he's my playmate every day,
He's got to feel better
So we can play.

Mary's Griddle

Mary loves her electric griddle.
She grills and fries
Foods, big and little.

Pork chops, burgers, onions, and potatoes,
Bacon, omelets,
And green tomatoes.

She turns and turns and seasons just right.
Everything from the griddle
Is a taste delight!

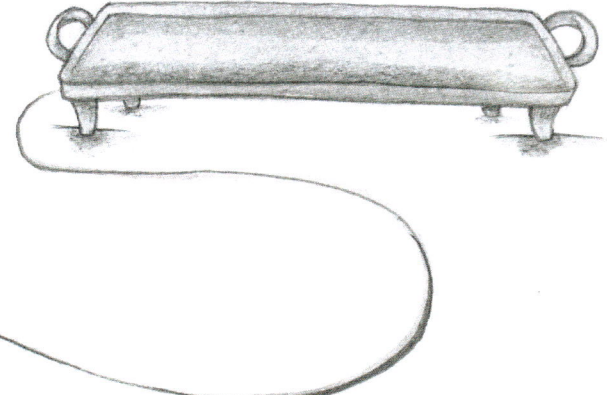

The Screen Door

The screen door swings to and fro
As it slaps and bangs,
Seeing folks come and go.

Sometimes it sways alone with the breeze,
Opening and closing
With the greatest of ease.

When we're at home,
Neighbors come every day.
Screen door never stays shut unless we're away.

Footprints

Footprints are seen everywhere in the sand.
They're tiny, they're big…
Miniscule and grand.

Some prints are paws from a dog on a leash.
Others are birds'
Little tiny feet.

My Mom's prints show all of her toes,
But Dad has on shoes…
Just why, I don't know.

Twisting and turning to see my own prints,
I fall in the sand
Then run for the rinse.

Lancer

Lancer is a white horse that has a fluffy tail.
He likes to trot and gallop
Along a quiet trail.

When he goes to the horseshows, he's brushed and neatly groomed.
With his head held high,
A champion's posture he has assumed.

He goes through his paces and sails over the rails.
He's beautiful to watch
And his strength never fails.

St. Patrick's Day

All the leprechauns are out today.
They know it's a green
Kind of holiday.

Shamrocks and great big pots of gold…
Oh, the tales those elves
Have told!

St. Patrick's Day is March seventeen.
You don't want to get pinched,
So you'd better wear green.

Ricky Raccoon

Ricky Raccoon is big and fat.
His tail is striped and can
Act like a bat.

He sniffs and searches what food you've left
Then grabs it, eats it,
And leaves a mess.

Ricky comes out mostly at night.
He has no fear and can
Quickly take flight.

Don't leave any food for this guy to eat
Because he'll stay with you
'til you give him heat!

Cluffy

My kitty cat's name is Cluffy.
She's copper and white
And oh so fluffy.

She sleeps and stretches and scratches the chair.
She rubs on my leg,
But I don't care.

She's pretty and sweet and softly mews
'Til I give her a treat
Or maybe a few.

Cluffy and I really like to play.
If I could stay home from school,
We'd play all day.

CPSIA information can be obtained
at www.ICGtesting.com
Printed in the USA
273350LV00005B